Monster Stew

by Jennifer Eyen

To Gregory

Published by Willowisp Press, Inc.
401 E. Wilson Bridge Road, Worthington, Ohio 43085

Copyright © 1990 by Willowisp Press, Inc.

Printed in the United States of America
10 9 8 7 6 5 4 3 2 1

ISBN 0-87406-436-8

Contents

A Creepy Night

It was a creepy night. The wind was creepy. My dog was creepy. My parents looked creepy. Even my dinner was creepy—corned beef and turnip stew with lima beans. My mom and dad made me eat nine bites, because I'm nine years old. That's the rule in our house.

I tried to feed my bites of stew to my dog. But when I held out a spoonful of stew to him, he just whined and ran away into the living room. Even my dog won't eat Mom's corned beef and turnip stew with lima beans.

My older brother looked creepy, too. He always looks creepy. But tonight he looked especially creepy because he's the only one in our family who likes the stew. He loves it. He's eleven years old, but he probably ate about eleven hundred bites. He would have eaten

more, too, but he ate so much he got sick and had to go to bed early.

I had a weird feeling that tonight wasn't just any old night. Tonight something was going to happen—maybe something terrible. Maybe I had this feeling because of the corned beef and turnip stew with lima beans.

I thought I heard something when I was walking up the stairs. But it was only my dad gargling in the bathroom.

Then I thought I heard something when I was getting ready for bed. But it was only my mom running the garbage disposal down in the kitchen. I hoped she was grinding up the rest of that yucky stew.

I heard something when I was turning out the light. But it was only my brother burping in his room. He went to bed with a bad stomachache. Well, what did he think would happen if he ate so much of that awful stew?

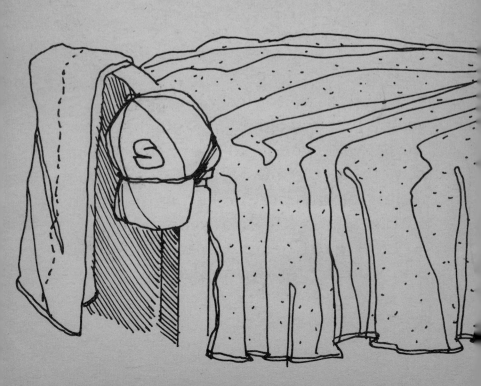

I couldn't sleep, so I sat on my bed and looked out the window. Clouds were blowing across the full moon. Creepy. The wind was blowing dead leaves up into the air, and the tree branches were waving around. Very creepy. My dog was down in the garden below my window. He was howling at the storm. It was the creepiest night in a long time!

I sat in my room thinking. The wind was blowing harder, and it had started to rain. The raindrops splattered against the roof. I listened to the sounds and stared out the window.

That's when I saw it. Up in the sky, in the clouds, by the full moon, I saw flashes of light. As I watched them, they seemed to come closer and closer. The lights were heading straight for our house.

Wait! What was that noise? It sounded very close, like it was right in our house. Like it was right in my room. Like it was right behind me.... Suddenly, I

felt something grab my shoul-
der!

"Aggrrhh!" I screamed.

"Aggrrhh!" another voice screamed.

11

Do You Believe in Monsters?

It was only my mother.

"What's the matter with you?" she asked me. "You scared the daylights out of me! I just came up to make sure your window was closed. There's a storm coming."

"Mom," I said pointing out the window, "there are white lights flashing in the sky!"

"That's only lightning," she said. "Now, hop into bed. It's late."

When Mom left my room, I hid my
head under my pillow. Crash! Boom!
The storm was really loud now.

At least Mom said it was a storm.
But how did I know that the booming
was really thunder? How did I know
that the lights were really lightning?
How did I know that the splatter on the
roof was really raindrops?

Maybe the flashes I saw were the
landing lights of a spaceship. Maybe

the booms I heard were the spaceship's
engines. Maybe the splatter on the roof
was a secret ray the spaceship shot at
my house.

"Help!" I yelled as loud as I could
from under my pillow. "Monsters from
space are attacking our house!"

I heard the booms and saw the lights
flash.

"Arrgghh!" I yelled again.

Dad came running into my room. "Are you okay?" he asked. "Are you afraid of the storm?"

Am I afraid of the storm? No. Am I afraid of space monsters? Yes. Definitely yes. But how could I explain that to Dad?

"No," I said. "I'm not afraid of the storm."

Dad stood and looked at me. "Well?" he said.

"Dad," I said, "do you believe in monsters from outer space?"

He smiled. "No, but I do believe in monsters from inner space," he said.

"Inner space?" I asked. "What do you mean?"

"I mean your imagination," he said, pointing to his head. "I think maybe you were having a bad dream. Now, please, go to sleep."

Just then we heard a strange knocking sound coming from outside.

"Did you hear that?" I whispered pulling the blankets up to my chin.

"Yes, it's a branch tapping against the window," answered Dad. "Now, good night."

Dad gave me a hug and stood up. Then he walked out and closed the door.

Go Back to Sleep

I lay back down on my bed. But I couldn't sleep. I pulled the covers over my head. But I could still see the lights outside my window. They seemed awfully close now. And the booms were getting louder, too.

When the lights got so bright I couldn't stand it anymore, I screamed, "THE SPACE MONSTERS ARE COMING!"

I rolled with my covers into a huge lump. I fell backward out of bed and onto the floor with a loud bump.

This time Mom came rushing into my room. "Is that you there on the floor?" she asked. "What's the matter now?"

I felt a little silly lying in a big lump on the floor with my blankets wound around my head.

I had rug fuzz in my mouth. I spit it out and said, "Mom, they're here. Just look out the window and tell me what they look like."

"Tell you what who looks like?" she asked, looking out the window. "There's nothing out there except the swing set and jungle gym."

"But, Mom," I said, "I heard them."

"Heard who?" she asked.

"The space monsters," I told her. "I heard their spaceship and saw the lights."

"Now listen," she said. "If you don't get into bed and go to sleep right now, you're going to be in big trouble."

"But, Mom..." I started.

"Not another word!" she said as she walked out and closed the door.

It was no use. She didn't believe me. How could she not see the spaceship? It had to be right there in the backyard.

I hid under my blankets for a little while, trying not to think about what was in the backyard. Finally, I thought I heard the sound of someone walking around. I knew it had to be the space creatures walking around in the spaceship.

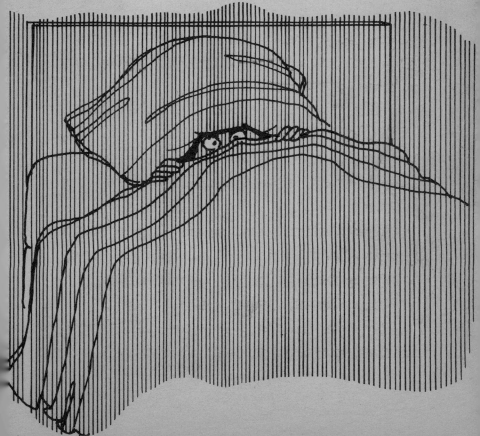

I pulled my blanket off the bed and wrapped it around me. I crawled to the window. The lights were very bright. I took a deep breath and peeked out my window.

There's Something
in the Backyard!

I couldn't believe my eyes! The backyard was lighted with bright flashing lights! And the lights were coming from a little silver spaceship that had landed right in Mom's flowers!

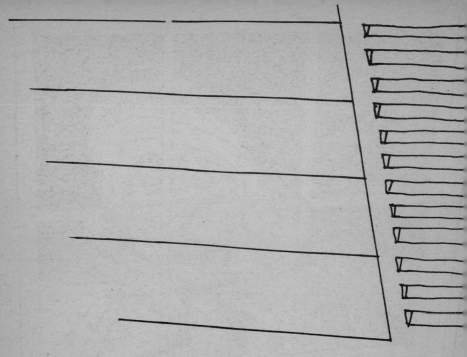

What could I do?

Mom and Dad wouldn't believe me. And they were asleep. My brother was in bed with a bad stomachache from eating too much corned beef and turnip stew with lima beans. My dog was a big chicken. Besides, if he barked at the space creatures they might get mad and blast him with their space ray.

There was only one person left. And that was me! I had to go down and meet the space creatures.

I put on my shoes and bathrobe. I looked at myself in the mirror. I didn't look very tough. The problem was that my bathrobe was fuzzy and yellow and had some cartoon characters on it. I really needed to look tough. I was going to meet some space creatures, and you have to look tough for that!

Just then, I saw my Halloween mask in the closet. My brother and I were monsters for Halloween last year. He has a mask just like mine. It's green, with lots of big warts and two big ugly white eyes. It's really gross. If somebody ever made a mask out of corned beef and turnip stew with lima beans, it would look like my Halloween mask.

I put on the mask and looked in the mirror. That's better, I told myself. I felt a lot tougher. I took a deep breath and opened my bedroom door. It made a little squeak, like it always does. But nobody heard it. Then I slowly walked down the stairs.

When I reached the bottom, I listened. Did I hear noises coming from the kitchen? I sneaked up as close to the kitchen door as I could.

Yes! I did hear some strange, quiet

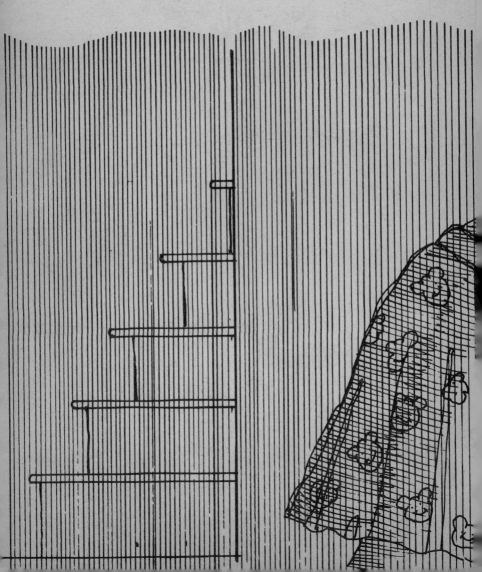

slurping noises. It sounded a little like my dog drinking out of his water dish.

I had to look. My legs were shaking. Checking to see if my mask was still on okay, I bent down and slowly opened the kitchen door just a bit.

Space Monsters
and Lima Beans

There it was!

It was just a little taller than me. It was green and had great big white eyes. And can you guess what it was doing in the kitchen?

The creature had opened up our refrigerator and was gulping the corned beef and turnip stew right out of the bowl! It was making the slurping noises that I'd heard.

The creature must have picked all
the lima beans out of the bowl. He stuck
them on his head. There was greasy
stew all over his green face. There was
greasy stew all over his fingers. Yuck!
I don't know which was worse—the
creature or the stew.

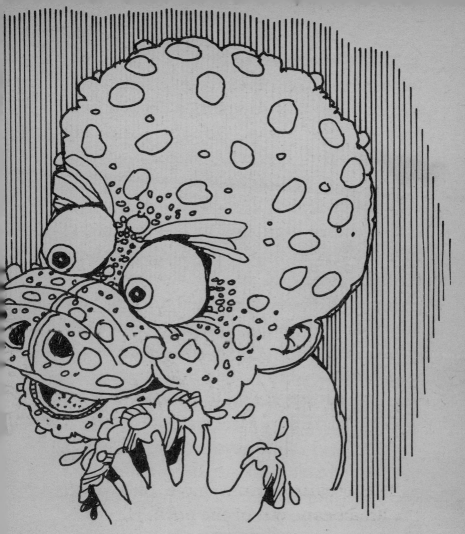

He kept poking into the pan and slop-
ping the stuff into his mouth. The worst
thing was I could tell he loved the stew.
He was slurping it up like it was the
best thing he had ever eaten.

That's how I knew he was a creature from outer space. Nobody on Earth could eat that much of my mom's corned beef and turnip stew. Nobody but my brother—and I knew he was upstairs in bed with a stomachache.

I didn't know what to do. Here was a real space creature in our house. It had landed in our backyard, and now it was eating out of our refrigerator.

For a second, I wanted to run upstairs and get Mom and Dad. But they wouldn't believe there was a creature from outer space eating our stew. They would just tell me to go back to bed.

Just then, the kitchen door made a squeak, and the creature looked over at me. My heart almost stopped as the creature stared at me. I stared back at his weird white eyes and his green skin, all covered with lima beans.

What would happen now?

Welcome to Earth

The creature stared at me. He looked at my mask for a long time. Maybe he was frightened of it. Maybe I looked a little *too* tough.

But he wasn't scared of my mask after all. He just made a noise that

41

sounded a lot like a burp. I thought it must be the stew that made him burp.

Then the creature turned back around and reached into the bowl. He pulled out a big greasy piece of corned beef and stuffed it into his mouth. Gross me out!

That's when I noticed the creature looked a lot like my Halloween mask.

He was green and had big white eyes.
And he wasn't sticking the lima beans
on his head. They were green warts,
just like on my mask!

I decided to try to talk to him. He
didn't seem mean or dangerous. He just

seemed hungry. The way he ate the stew made me think he didn't have very good manners. Only my creepy brother eats stew with his fingers!

I checked my mask and stood up. I walked into the kitchen toward the space creature.

"Welcome to Earth," I said. I knew it was dumb, but I couldn't think of anything else to say.

He looked at me for a second and then went back to eating Mom's stew.

I coughed. "Umm," I said, "Welcome to the planet Earth. Where are you from? Do you like our food?"

The creature turned around and made a funny little sound. Then he did something really horrible. He held out the bowl of stew to me and offered me a big greasy turnip.

I almost got sick looking at the turnip. Thinking about eating more of the stew made me feel like I was going to faint—or throw up. My face felt hot and sweaty. I couldn't breathe. I had to take

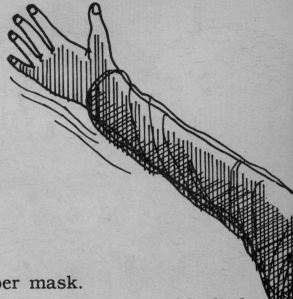

off my rubber mask.

Then the creature turned and looked at me again. But when he saw my real face instead of the mask, his big white eyes got even bigger. He started to tremble all over. Then he threw up his arms in fear. He was terrified of my real face!

The stew bowl fell on the floor. He started to make a squeaking sound. Then he yelled.

"Wahhhhhh!" he screamed.

"Arrgghh!" I screamed.

We just stood there for a second screaming at each other. Then he ran right out the back door. And I ran upstairs to my room!

I looked out my window just in time to see the spaceship taking off. It was gone in the blink of an eye.

I jumped into my bed and pulled the covers over my head. I squeezed my eyes shut. But I could still see the ugly creature holding out that greasy turnip to me!

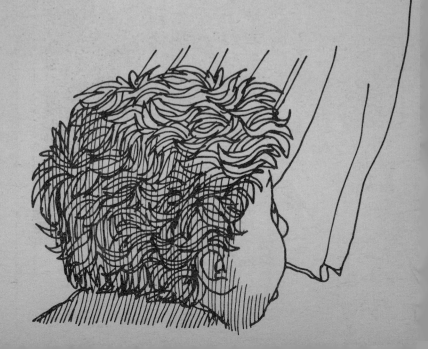

No More Stew!

I woke up the next morning, and the sun was shining. I heard voices in the backyard below my window.

I went over to my window and looked out. There were my mom, dad, and brother standing by the flower garden. The dog was with them.

"It looks like the dog has been sleeping on your flowers again," Dad said. "A bunch of them are smashed."

Mom shook her head. "I guess so," she said. "Something funny was going on around here last night."

"Yes," said Dad. "The flowers are smashed, and the stew is all eaten."

When Dad mentioned the stew, my brother said quickly, "I bet the dog ate the stew, too. He smashed the flowers and ate up the stew. Bad dog!" he said to the dog.

"Wait!" I shouted down from the window. "I know what happened last night!"

I ran downstairs and met them in the backyard. "A space creature ate the stew. First he landed his spaceship in the flowers and smashed them. Then he came in and ate all the stew," I explained as fast as I could. "I saw him. I talked to him."

My brother gave me a funny look. Mom and Dad just shook their heads and smiled.

"I think that was all just a bad dream," Mom said.

"Don't you remember?" added Dad. "I came into your room and talked to you. You were afraid of the storm."

"No," I said. "I wasn't afraid of the storm. And it wasn't just a dream. The creature looked like our Halloween masks, all green and warty. He offered me some of the stew, but I wouldn't eat any of it."

Mom and Dad started laughing. Dad
put his arm around me. "That's a great
story," he said. "Imagine a creature from
outer space coming all the way to our
planet just to eat your mom's stew."

When he said the word stew, Dad made a face. He pretended to stick his finger down his throat. Mom gave him a dirty look. "But it was just a dream," said Dad.

"Yeah," said my brother, "you just had a bad dream."

I knew they wouldn't believe me. They thought I had a bad dream—a corned beef and turnip stew nightmare. We all started to walk into the house to eat breakfast when I thought of something.

"Wait a minute!" I shouted. "The dog didn't eat the stew. He hates the stew as much as I do! He wouldn't eat the stew if it was the last thing on Earth!"

When I talked about the stew, the dog put his tail between his legs and whimpered.

Mom and Dad stopped walking and looked at me. I could tell they were thinking about what I had said. Then they looked at the dog. My brother kept walking into the kitchen.

Mom looked back at the smashed flowers. I patted the dog's head. Mom and Dad were quiet for a long time, standing on the back porch.

Finally, Dad said to me, "You're right. The dog doesn't like the stew. You don't like the stew, and I don't like the stew."

Then Mom said with a smile, "You know what? I don't even like the stew very much. I just made it because I thought you all liked it!"

Inside the house, I heard my brother opening the refrigerator door to get some milk for his cereal.

Then Dad said, "That means there are only two creatures in the whole universe who like corned beef and turnip stew with lima beans."

"You're right," Mom answered. "One of them is a monster who visited us in his spaceship last night."

"And the other one is eating cereal in the kitchen!" Dad added.

We all laughed and laughed. The dog wagged his tail and barked.

"Maybe I won't make the stew again for a while," Mom said.

"That's a good idea," said Dad. "No more monster stew!"

RECIPE FOR MONSTER STEW

Ingredients

1 pound of greasy corned beef
12 big dirty turnips
2 cups of slimy green lima beans
6 cups of water that you just washed
    your gym socks in
salt, pepper

1. Cut the corned beef up into little
pieces, and put them in a large pot.
2. Throw the turnips and lima beans

onto the floor. Step on them. Then throw them in the pot.

3. Add the water to the pot. If you forget to take out the socks you just washed, don't worry.

4. Boil the stew as long as you can, until the smell starts to make you sick. (Not longer than one month!)

5. Remove the lima beans from the stew, and stick them on your head, like the space creature does in *Monster Stew*.

6. Offer the rest of the stew to your dog. If he whines and runs away, you know you've made a great batch of MONSTER STEW!

7. Serve the stew to your creepiest brother or sister.

ABOUT THE AUTHOR

Jennifer Eyen started writing even before she could read. As a little girl, she used to make squiggles on paper and pretend to "read" them to her mom.

Jennifer writes poetry and grown-up stuff, too. But she especially likes to write children's stories. When she's not writing, she likes traveling, going to movies, and eating out at nice restaurants. Jennifer used to cook at home. But she had to stop because she couldn't keep hungry space creatures out of her refrigerator.

Jennifer lives in Columbus with her husband, son, and a very silly basset hound.